Betty the Yeti

AND HER DANCING FEET

by Mandy R. Marx

illustrated by Antonella Fant

PICTURE WINDOW BOOKS
a capstone imprint

Published by Picture Window Books, an imprint of Capstone
1710 Roe Crest Drive, North Mankato, Minnesota 56003
capstonepub.com

Library of Congress Cataloging-in-Publication Data is available on the Library
of Congress website.
ISBN: 9781484682562 (hardcover)
ISBN: 9781484682524 (paperback)
ISBN: 9781484682531 (ebook pdf)

Summary: It's time for the school's winter concert. Betty the Yeti is excited! But
what happens when Betty's dancing feet do more than keep the beat?

Designer: Hilary Wacholz

TABLE OF CONTENTS

MEET BETTY AND HER FAMILY 4

Chapter 1
BETTY SINGS 7

Chapter 2
CONCERT PRACTICE 12

Chapter 3
A GLITCH IN THE PLAN 20

Chapter 4
DANCING FEET KEEP THE BEAT 26

MEET BETTY AND HER FAMILY

Betty Yeti and her family moved from a cold mountain home to an apartment in the city. Mama Yeti, Betty, and her twin brothers, Eddy and Freddy, are the only yetis in town. Getting used to a new place is hard. But it's especially hard when you're a yeti who isn't quite ready to stand out.

Mama

Eddy

Betty

Freddy

Chapter 1
BETTY SINGS

Betty Yeti sang as she got ready for school. Her mind was on her school's upcoming winter concert.

When Betty saw snowflakes out the window, her excitement grew. Betty loved snow almost as much as she loved music.

Betty sang and danced into the kitchen. Her brothers sat eating breakfast.

"You're in a good mood, sis," said Freddy.

"Look at those dancing feet!"
said Eddy.

Betty twirled and laughed with
her brothers. It was fun to be silly
with them.

In music class that day, Betty couldn't wait to sing with her classmates. But she worried about controlling her dancing feet.

Betty often felt shy at school.
She didn't like lots of people
looking at her.

Chapter 2

CONCERT PRACTICE

Over the next week, the children learned their songs. Betty liked the song about snowflakes best.

Once in a while, Betty's toes tapped. But she would quickly catch herself and stop.

During one song, everyone had to clap to the beat. Betty found the beat easily. Her classmates . . . did not.

Mrs. Carter noticed. "Let's try again," she said. "And this time, watch Betty."

Betty didn't like everyone looking at her.

The music started again. Betty

sang nervously. She clapped to

the beat. Her classmates watched.

But they still couldn't get it.

Without thinking, Betty's dancing feet kicked in. She stomped when she clapped. Her classmates felt it. They picked up the beat!

"Yes, Betty," cried Mrs. Carter. "Stomp those feet! That's it, children!"

Betty smiled. She still didn't like everyone looking at her. But she was proud she could help.

For the next week, the children practiced. During the last song, Betty stomped to the beat.

Chapter 3

A GLITCH IN THE PLAN

The week of the concert arrived.

"Today we'll practice on the risers," Mrs. Carter said. "Shortest children stand in front. Tallest in the back."

Betty stood on the back riser. "Oh, Betty," said Mrs. Carter. "I'm afraid you're too tall back there."

Everyone turned to look at
Betty. She wanted to shrink.

"Let's put you on the bottom
row, Betty," said Mrs. Carter.
"We just won't have anyone
stand behind you."

Practice began. Soon, the class
got to the clapping song. Betty
stomped her feet.

The risers shook with every stomp of Betty's big feet! Her classmates bounced up and down. Some lost their balance.

The class tried again without Betty's stomp. But they lost the beat. Mrs. Carter thought for a moment. Her eyes lit up. "I've got it!" she cried.

Chapter 4

DANCING FEET KEEP THE BEAT

On the day of the concert, people filled the auditorium. Betty's class sang the first few songs. People took pictures and videos. They clapped politely.

Finally, Mrs. Carter said, "For this last song, we have Betty Yeti on the drums!"

Betty sat behind a red drum kit.
She took a breath to calm herself.
Then she counted off, "One, two,
three, four!"

Betty stomped the drum pedal
to the beat.

The children sang and clapped. They sounded great!

The song ended. Everyone cheered. Freddy Yeti shouted, "Yay for Betty and her dancing feet!"

Glossary

auditorium (aw-duh-TOR-ee-uhm)—a room, hall, or building used for public gatherings

glitch (GLICH)—a problem that causes a small setback

pedal (PED-uhl)—a lever that can be pushed to make something happen; tapping the foot pedal of a kick drum makes a booming sound

practice (PRAK-tiss)—to keep working to improve a skill

riser (RYE-zuhr)—a wide platform built like stairs so that performers can be seen better

Talk About It

1. Betty felt excited about the concert. But she felt nervous about people watching her. Have you ever experienced something that made you feel both nervous and excited? What was it?

2. Betty loves music, so music class is one of her favorite classes. Describe your favorite class.

3. Betty was nervous about leading her class clapping, but she didn't want to let her teacher down. Would you feel nervous in that situation? Why or why not?

Write About It

1. It was Mrs. Carter's idea to have Betty use a kick drum to keep the beat. What if you were the teacher? Write about what ideas you might have had to help the class.

2. Betty is silly with her brothers. But she is serious at school. Do you act differently at home than you do at school? Write about one way you're different in those two places.

3. Betty could have said no to playing the drums. Write about why you think she didn't. What does that tell you about Betty's personality?

About the Author

Mandy R. Marx is a writer and editor. She lives in a chilly town in Minnesota with her husband, daughter, and a white, silky haired pup. She has a curious mind and stays on the lookout for yetis. In her spare time, Mandy enjoys singing, laughing with friends and family, and walking her pup through what she suspects is a magical forest.

About the Illustrator

María Antonella Fant is a visual designer, children's book illustrator, and concept artist. Her illustrations reflect her childish, restless, and curious personality, taking inspiration from animated cartoons and children's books from her childhood. María enjoys the way a child thinks, drawing like them and for them. María was born, and currently lives, in Argentina.